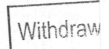 flyers

FLYER books are for confident readers
who can take on the challenge of
a longer story.

Can YOU spot the aeroplane
hidden in the story?

To my Mum, Tess McHale –
for the love, the sense of humour
and approximately 10,000 dinners.

CONOR MCHALE was born in Dublin in 1969. By day he is an archaeologist, a job which involves reconstructing past human civilisations while standing in mucky holes. By night he writes and illustrates books for children, a job which thankfully doesn't involve any mud. He lives in Dublin with his wife, Susannah, and their son, Oscar. He has also written and illustrated *Jigsaw Stew* and *Fishbum and Splat* for the O'Brien Press FLYERS series.

Don't Open that Box!

Written and illustrated by
Conor McHale

THE O'BRIEN PRESS
DUBLIN

First published 2001 by The O'Brien Press Ltd,
12 Terenure Road East, Rathgar, Dublin 6, Ireland.
Tel: +353 1 4923333; Fax: +353 1 4922777
E-mail: books@obrien.ie
Website: www.obrien.ie
Reprinted 2002, 2004, 2007.

ISBN: 978-0-86278-705-9

British Library Cataloguing-in-Publication Data
A catalogue reference for this book is available from the
British Library.

4   5   6   7   8   9   10
07   08   09   10   11   12

The O'Brien Press receives
assistance from

Typesetting, editing, layout, design: The O'Brien Press Ltd
Printing: Cox & Wyman Ltd

CHAPTER 1

Two Boxes 6

CHAPTER 2

Greta 19

CHAPTER 3

Run! 25

CHAPTER 4

Splinters 35

CHAPTER 5

Or Was She? 42

CHAPTER 6

A Week Later 58

Two Boxes

The postman had just delivered **two** boxes. One was big, the other small. Granny Lambert peered through her glasses. 'I wonder who sent them?' she said.

Her pet cat Belzoni sniffed. Something smelt **odd**.

'Ooh!' said Granny Lambert, 'look what it says on the big one.'

Belzoni began making a **fuss**. He
had read the label on the smaller one.

DON'T OPEN
THAT BOX!
OPEN THIS
ONE INSTEAD

It was no good. Granny
Lambert had already opened the
huge one . . .

A **crocodile** leapt out. His jaws sprang open. SNAP! Granny Lambert was in his mouth. GULP! She was gone!

Belzoni squealed and leapt onto the highest thing he could find.

The crocodile burped and picked what was left of Granny Lambert from between his **teeth**.

'And now for **dessert**,' grunted the crocodile.

'Stay away from me, you jumped-up handbag!' howled Belzoni, 'and don't bother trying to push the clock over, it's bolted to the wall.'

'What a pity,' snorted the crocodile. 'Still, you'll have to come down some time and I can **wait**.' He turned and disappeared through the kitchen door.

'What ... what is going on?' said Belzoni. 'Poor Granny Lambert. That was some **surprise**! I hope it's the last surprise for today.'

It wasn't.

The smaller cardboard box
(the one Granny Lambert had
never opened) began to shake
and bounce. Belzoni's fur stood
on end. Whatever was in it was
trying to get **out** . . .

The box rattled around the hall. It battered the furniture and knocked against the walls. It didn't stop rolling until the lid fell off and out **popped** . . .

... a chicken.

Belzoni hopped down off the clock.
He had never been afraid of chickens
before and he was in no mood to
start.

CHAPTER 2

Greta

'What is going on here?' asked Belzoni.

'They call me Greta,' said the chicken. 'I'm from the **zoo**, and so is that alli–, em, crocodile. He escaped last week by post. When the other animals discovered he was gone they chose me to follow him.'

'Wow! You must be the bravest animal in the zoo,' said Belzoni.

'Not really,' said Greta, 'I was the only one who could fit in the box.'

'Oh dear,' mumbled Belzoni. 'So why does he travel by post?'

'It's a great way of **ambushing** people,' answered Greta.

'So far, he's eaten loads of people with that box. I always arrive too late. All I find is an empty house, everyone gobbled. Is he still here?'

'I think so,' said Belzoni.

'We have to **stop** him,' whispered Greta as she opened the kitchen door and looked in. 'Hmm, I can't see him, can you?'

'Er, yes,' said Belzoni.

'Where?' asked Greta.

CHAPTER 3

Run!

'Run!' shouted Greta. They darted
away as the crocodile pounced,
his teeth only a **foot** from their
tails.

'To the stairs!' she cried. The crocodile's jaws snapped so close to their heels they could smell **Granny** off his breath.

'Up, up, up!' And up they flew with the crocodile almost nibbling their elbows.

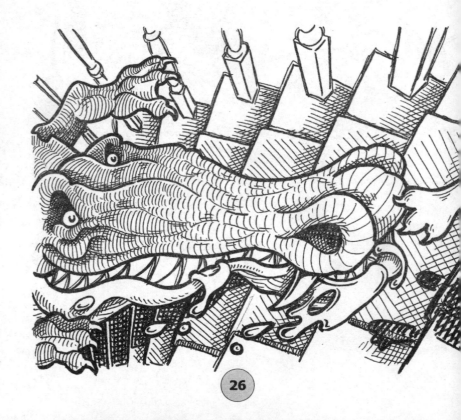

'To the bedroom!' Greta shouted. They shot across the landing with the crocodile **snap, snap, snapping** all the way.

Belzoni's heart raced as they leapt up onto the bed.

'What do we do now?' asked
Belzoni. 'Hit him with a pillow?'

They were **cornered**. The crocodile
stood at the end of the bed. Slowly he
opened his jaws wide enough to
swallow the pillow, wide enough to
swallow the mattress, wide enough to
swallow the whole bed – and them
with it.

'Goodbye, puss,' said Greta.

'**Wait!** I have an idea,'
whispered Belzoni. 'When I say
"Jump" . . .'

The crocodile lunged as
Belzoni and Greta jumped clear.
GULP! The bed disappeared.

By the time the crocodile realised
he couldn't taste cat or chicken (only
springs and sheets), Belzoni and Greta
were gone.

'Quickly, **hide** in the garden shed,'
said Belzoni.

They waited there until nightfall.

CHAPTER 4

Splinters

'Greta,' said Belzoni, 'that bed **was** wooden, wasn't it?'

'Yes,' said Greta.

'When he goes to the toilet do you think he'll get splinters?'

'I do hope so,' said Greta. 'Now, follow me.'

They crept out of the shed and up to the hall door. The huge box was sitting on the step.

'I knew it,' whispered Greta. 'He's inside waiting for the postman to collect him.

'**Look!** These are all the people
he's eaten so far. The one at the
bottom is his next feed.'

'Mr Bracket's address is from Granny Lambert's address book,' she explained. 'He **always** picks his next victim out of his last victim's address book. It's how I've been able to follow him. His claw mark is on the address of his next meal.

'Now we need to change this address to some place where he can't do any harm. **Where** will we send– ?'

Mr. T. Bracket
Short Street
Longford

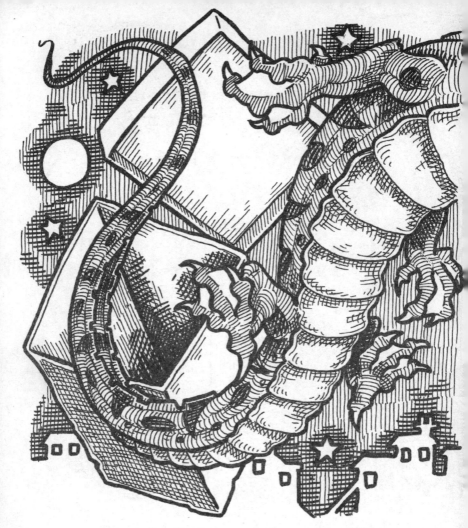

'**Gotcha**!' shouted the crocodile, leaping out of the box. His jaws sprang open. **SNAP!** Greta was in his mouth. **GULP!** She was gone!

Belzoni was **dumbstruck**.

Greta was gone. Greta was gone,
gone, gone.

CHAPTER 5

Or Was She?

The crocodile grabbed Belzoni. 'You're **next**!' he said with a nasty smile full of razor-sharp teeth.

Then he coughed. He stopped smiling and he coughed. He let go of Belzoni and he coughed. He grabbed his throat, lay on his back and coughed. Cough, cough, cough!

Cough! **GAAACK!** Greta shot out of his mouth like a rocket and landed on the roof.

Belzoni scrambled up the drainpipe after her. She was dazed and she was covered in crocodile drool, but otherwise she was fine.

'He must be **allergic** to feathers,' said Belzoni.

Greta was alive and the crocodile couldn't possibly follow them onto the roof. Belzoni suddenly felt very brave.

He felt **so** good he never
noticed the crocodile walking to
the back-garden shed. He never
noticed the crocodile taking a
ladder out. He never noticed the
crocodile leaning it against the
house and climbing up.

He **only** noticed when the
crocodile's head appeared at the end
of the roof.

'I may be allergic to feathers but I'm not allergic to fur,' snarled the crocodile. 'And, anyway, I can always **pluck** your friend before I eat her!'

They were cornered again. But
jumping off a bed to escape was **very**
different from jumping off a roof.

Belzoni grabbed Greta and ran towards the chimney. The crocodile hissed and began to run. His **claws** clattered and scattered tiles as he charged towards them.

Belzoni scrambled onto the chimney stack and pulled Greta up after him.

The crocodile's teeth shone like **daggers** as he steam-rollered forward. His hot breath hit Belzoni like a wall. It made him stagger and slip and fall.

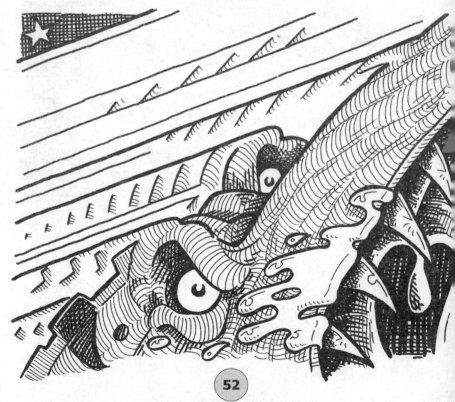

Right down the **chimney**.

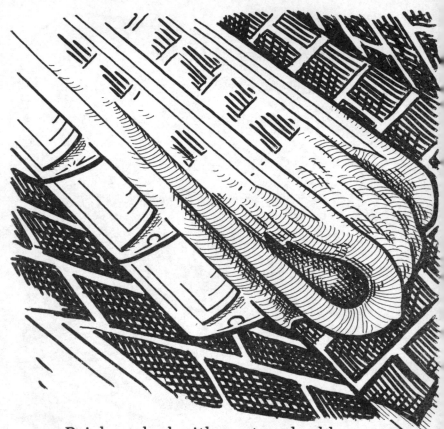

Bricks caked with soot rushed by
Belzoni's nose. He looked up at the
moon. It disappeared and was
replaced by a mouth full of sharp
curled teeth – the crocodile had
thrown himself in after them.

Belzoni hugged Greta.

'Goodbye, chuck,' he whimpered.

The teeth plummeted closer
and closer until **BOOM!**

Everything went jet black.

Belzoni opened his eyes. He was with Greta in Granny Lambert's sitting room. The crocodile had been knocked out **cold**.

Greta was still dazed. 'Is that you, Santa?' she said to the crocodile.

'No, it's not Santa,' said Belzoni. 'But you've just given me an **idea**. Quick, let's get him into that box!'

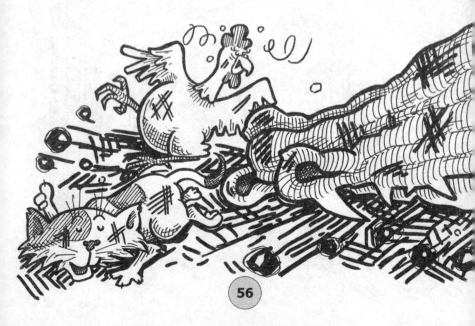

A Week Later

Belzoni was writing on a box – a box big enough for a cat and a chicken. They were posting themselves on a holiday – a **long** one.

'I was so dazed at the time,' said Greta, 'I never noticed where you sent the crocodile.'

'I posted him to a place where he can't do any more harm,' said Belzoni. 'The next time he leaps out of that box . . .

. . . he's in for a big **surprise.'**

'Where are you posting **us**?' asked Greta.

'I think I'll let the post office decide that. I'll give them all the **information** they need on the box.'

'Let's get in,' said Belzoni.

'What happens if we get
hungry on the way?' asked Greta.

'Well, I don't know about you,'
said Belzoni . . .

'. . . but there's enough **chicken** in here to last me a month!'